Miffy's Happy New Year!

Dick Bruna

Big Tent Entertainment
216 West 18th Street
New York, NY 10011

Published in 2004 by Big Tent Entertainment. Design © copyright Big Tent Entertainment.
Publication licensed by Mercis Publishing bv, Amsterdam, through Big Tent Entertainment.
Based upon the television series Miffy and Friends. Miffy and Friends based on the work of Dick Bruna.
Illustrations Dick Bruna © copyright Mercis bv, 1953-2004. © copyright Mercis Media bv, all rights reserved.
Library of Congress control number: Available from the Library of Congress. ISBN: 1-59226-233-3
Printed in China.
2 4 6 8 10 9 7 5 3

It was the last day of school before vacation, and Miffy's class was busy drawing pictures about winter. Aggie drew a yellow sleigh. Winnie made a tree with snow on it. Melanie worked on a hat and a yellow scarf. And Miffy drew a picture of a snow bunny!

When the bell rang for recess, Aggie, Winnie, Melanie and Miffy rushed outside. There was snow everywhere!

The girls talked about their holiday plans.

"We're celebrating the new year with our families," Aggie and Winnie said.

"I'm staying at Miffy's house," Melanie said. "I'm so excited."

"Me, too!" said Miffy.

When the girls were back in the classroom, Miffy came up with a great idea.

"Melanie, let's have a party on New Year's Day. We'll use our winter drawings as invitations and bring them to Grunty, Poppy Pig, and Aunt Alice!"

"Yes," said Melanie, "and to Snuffy and Boris and Barbara, too."

On the back of her drawing, Miffy stamped a big number 1 for the first day of the new year. She added some colorful stars, too.

Miffy and Melanie made four invitations. Then with a long piece of ribbon, they attached the invitations to four big balloons. There was one for Poppy Pig and Grunty, one for Boris and Barbara Bear, one for Snuffy, and one for Aunt Alice, too.

After school, the girls jumped on their scooters and started for home. The wind blew the balloons this way and that. Miffy and Melanie held on tightly to the ribbons.

Suddenly Melanie's scooter hit a bump, and she let go of her balloons!

"Oh, no!" gasped Miffy, and she let go of her balloons, too!
"Melanie, are you all right?"
"I'm okay," said Melanie, "but our invitations are gone!"
"I know, but I'm glad you're not hurt," Miffy said.

That night Poppy Pig and Grunty were just finishing a bedtime story when Grunty jumped up.

"Poppy!" cried Grunty, "I think I saw something outside! It was round and white."

Poppy opened the door and looked out. She looked to the right and she looked to the left. She didn't see anything, so she went outside and walked around the whole house.

"There's nothing outside, and now it's time for bed. Good night, Grunty," said Poppy.

"Good night, Poppy," said Grunty.

Outside the wind started blowing harder.

"Poppy! Wake up!" Grunty whispered. "There is something outside."

Poppy woke up and saw a shadow move across the room.

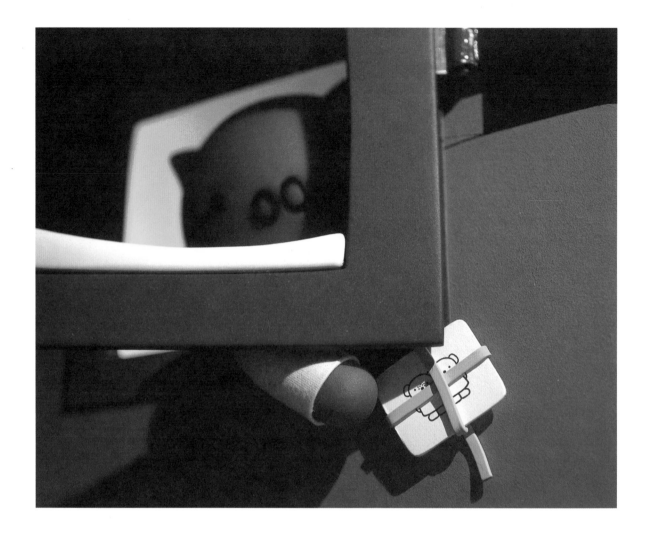

Poppy crept up to the window and reached out.
"It's a balloon and an envelope," Poppy laughed.
Then Poppy and Grunty saw the picture of Boris and Barbara.
"I think Boris and Barbara are inviting us to a New Year's party," said Poppy.
"How wonderful!" said Grunty.
"Yes, but we'd better get some sleep!" Poppy replied.

Three bright balloons fly through the night
High above where Miffy sleeps tight
Now the red one flies away
Leaving two balloons to stay
One red balloon, off in the night
Floats to the first ray of light

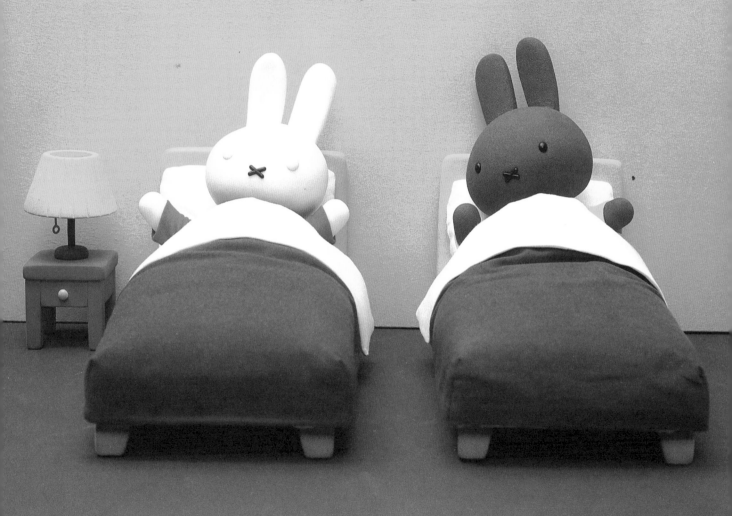

The next morning, Boris and Barbara decorated their living room for the holiday.

"Boris," said Barbara, "will you please go outside and get some logs from the pile?"

"Yes, of course," said Boris, and he went out at once.

Suddenly Boris heard a dog barking in the distance. He stopped and turned around. It sounded like Snuffy.

"Snuffy? Snuffy?" Boris called.

When Boris found Snuffy, she was barking at a red balloon high up in a tree.

"Hello, Snuffy," said Boris. "It looks like you found a pretty red balloon to play with. We'll need a ladder to get it out of there. Wait here and I'll get one."

Barbara helped Boris carry the ladder into the woods.

"Look!" said Barbara, "There's an invitation to a New Year's Day party tied to the balloon. But who's it from?"

"Hmmm, I suppose Snuffy knows where the party will be," answered Boris.

Snuffy wagged her tail. She was happy to have the balloon at last.

Across the woods, Miffy and Melanie helped Mother Bunny bake cookies for New Year's Day.

"When the cookies are in the oven, you can get ready for your dancing lesson at Aunt Alice's house," said Mother Bunny.

"Hooray! This holiday is so much fun," Miffy and Melanie cheered.

Soon the girls were practicing a special dance that Aunt Alice had taught them. While they were dancing, it started to snow again.

"Can we go out and play for a while?" Miffy asked.

"Of course," replied Aunt Alice.

As soon as the girls ran outside, Miffy saw something yellow under a bush.

"Look!" said Miffy. "It's the invitation we made for Aunt Alice."

"An invitation for me?" Aunt Alice sounded surprised.

"Yes! Will you come to our New Year's party tomorrow?" asked Miffy.

"Yes, thank you," Aunt Alice replied. "And thank you, clever yellow balloon for finding your way here all by yourself!"

 After their busy afternoon, Miffy and Melanie rested and ate the
cookies they had baked earlier.
 "Mmmm, these cookies are so good," said Melanie.
 Just when Miffy was going to answer Melanie, she heard noises
outside. "What's that?" she said.
 "Let's go outside and find out," Father Bunny suggested.

Snuffy, Boris, Barbara, Poppy, and Grunty were just arriving at Miffy's house.

The friends had met in the woods as Boris and Barbara were on their way to Miffy's, and Poppy and Grunty were on their way to Boris and Barbara's party.

"But, we're not giving a party," Barbara had said. "We think Miffy's having one, and I'm sure we're all welcome."

Just then Miffy, Melanie and Father Bunny walked outside.

"Happy New Year, Miffy!" shouted Boris.

"Happy New Year, Boris!" shouted Miffy. "What a nice surprise!"

Then they saw Aunt Alice coming toward the house.
"I've brought everyone a balloon," Aunt Alice said. "Make a wish
and let your balloon go."

Everyone counted: "Ten, nine, eight, seven, six, five, four, three, two, one, zero!"

All the balloons flew up toward the sky as Miffy and her friends called out, "Happy New Year!!"

Miffy watched the balloons float away.

"I wish all of my New Year's parties will be as good as this one!" she said.